# CHOOSE YOUR OWN ADVENTURE®

**Kids Love Reading
*Choose Your Own Adventure*®!**

---

"I like the way you can choose the way
the story goes."
**Beckett Kahn, age 7**

---

"If you don't read this book, you'll get payback."
**Amy Cook, age 8½**

---

"I thought this book was funny.
I think younger and older kids will like it."
**Tessa Jernigan, age 6½**

---

"This is fun reading. Once you go in to have an
adventure, you may never come out."
**Jude Fidel, age 7**

---

D1016486

Illustrated by Keith Newton
Book design by Peter Holm, Sterling Hill Productions
For information regarding permission, write to:

CHOOSECO
P.O. Box 46
Waitsfield, Vermont 05673
www.cyoa.com

A DRAGONLARK BOOK

ISBN-10: 1-937133-49-4
EAN: 978-1-937133-49-8

Published simultaneously in the United States and Canada

Printed in China

11 10 9 8 7 6 5 4 3 2 1

# CHOOSE YOUR OWN ADVENTURE®

# FIRE!

## R. A. MONTGOMERY

A DRAGONLARK BOOK

## READ THIS FIRST!!!

WATCH OUT!
THIS BOOK IS DIFFERENT
from every book you've ever read.

Do not read this book from the first page
through to the last page.
Instead, start on page 1 and read until you
come to your first choice. Then turn to the
page shown and see what happens.

When you come to the end of a story,
you can go back and start again.
Every choice leads to a new adventure.

Good luck!

This morning you've slept later than usual. When you go downstairs for breakfast, you know something is wrong. You smell smoke.

Black smoke is seeping out from under the kitchen door. You open the door.

*Turn to page 3.*

"Fire! Fire! The stove's on fire, Mom!"

There is no answer. You yell again, running out of the kitchen into the living room.

"Mom! It's burning. Help, Mom!"

Then you remember. Your mother went into town for the morning. Luckily, you memorized what she told you: "If there's a fire, get out of the house as fast as you can. Houses can be replaced. You can't."

"Where's my cat?" you ask yourself. Then you see the orange tiger-striped cat asleep on the couch.

"Come on, Nipper, let's get out of here!" you say.

*Turn to the next page.*

You grab the cat and dash out of the house into the summer sunshine.

"Help, someone! Help!" you yell. But there is no one around. "Help!" you cry again. The telephone is in the kitchen. You can't use that!

*Turn to page 6.*

You live in the country. The firehouse is about a mile and a half away. You have to go up a steep hill to get there. There is one house that's close to yours—the old Ryerson house.

*Turn to page 8.*

You've never actually seen old Mrs. Ryerson, but you've heard stories about her and the house. Stories about strange things— witches, ghosts, haunts.

*Go to the next page.*

"What do I do now?" you ask yourself as you let Nipper down on the grass.

What should you do? You can smell the smoke, even outdoors.

*If you decide to ride your bike to the firehouse, turn to page 10.*

*If you decide to run to Mrs. Ryerson's and try to phone the firehouse from there, turn to page 24.*

You decide to ride your bike, which is in the garage. You aren't supposed to ride it alone, but this is an emergency. You grab the bike, push it out onto the driveway, and hop on.

Wow! The smoke is really heavy now! What will your mom and dad think? Will they be mad?

*Turn to page 12.*

Just as you leave the driveway, Nipper skitters up a tree. He barely escapes getting wet from the lawn sprinkler. It's been a dry summer, and the grass is brown.

*Turn to page 14.*

"At least Nipper's safe," you say to yourself. Then you stop.

"Hey, maybe I can put the fire out myself! The hose is right there."

*If you decide to try to put the fire out yourself, turn to page 38.*

*If you decide to continue on to the firehouse, turn to page 42.*

"It won't hurt to answer," you think out loud. After all, you're outside in the sun.

You're all right.

You move forward a step and a half and open your mouth to speak. Nothing comes out.

"Don't be afraid. Come up to the porch," says the faint voice.

*Go on to the next page.*

Then you remember the fire and what you have to do. You must report the fire!

The voice speaks again. "You're from the house down the road, aren't you?"

*Turn to the next page.*

The front door is open, and you can see into the dark house. An old woman stands in the doorway behind the screen door. Her face and hair are white. Her bony, grayish hand holds the knob of the screen door and slowly pushes it open.

"Come in. Come in. I don't bite!"

*If you go up on the porch and talk with her, turn to page 32.*

*If you are too frightened to move, turn to page 54.*

"Watch out! Get out of the way! Move over there," yells a short, fat man in an oversized rubber coat and hat that almost hides his head.

"But the fire's in the kitchen, not the living room," you yell back at him. "You broke the wrong window!"

A large woman wearing the chief's hat says, "Listen to the kid. It's the kitchen, is it?"

You nod. The fire fighters break the window in the kitchen and pour streams of water into the kitchen. Several of the fire fighters rush inside.

Finally they come out of the house. The smoke has stopped, and so has the fire.

*Turn to page 23.*

"Well, everything's safe. Not quite as good as new, but not bad," the chief says to you and your mother. You look at the chief more carefully.

Why, it's Alice, who owns the bakery in town!

"Thanks, Alice. Thanks a lot," you say.

"Thanks, yourself," she says. "You're the one who told us the fire was in the kitchen. You'd make a good fire fighter. Ever thought of joining up? We can always use a good hand."

**The End**

You decide you'll never make it to the firehouse in time. You'll go to the Ryerson house.

Those are probably just stories about weird lights and faces at the windows. Nobody with any sense would believe them.

You run as fast as you can down the road and across the field, then across another field until you come to the house. It's an old three-story house with a big porch. The house looks gray and worn out.

"Mrs. Ryerson! Mrs. Ryerson? Help! Please help me," you yell. "My house is on fire!"

*Turn to page 26.*

Just before you reach the porch, you see a shadow by the front window next to the door. You slow down to a walk.

Suddenly you hear a faint, scary voice coming from inside the house.

"Come here. Don't be afraid."

You freeze in your tracks.

*If you decide to answer the voice, turn to page 16.*

*If you decide to run, turn to page 52.*

When you finally get to the top of the hill, you're out of breath and a little dizzy from working so hard.

"Wow, only a little bit farther," you say.

You zoom down the hill. The cool air rushing by feels good on your face and bare arms and legs.

All of a sudden you're there. The red brick firehouse sits between the school and a shopping center.

You peek through a window. No one is on duty!

What now?

---

*If you decide to run to one of the stores and ask for help, turn to page 45.*

*If you decide to try to sound the fire alarm, turn to page 49.*

"No, I don't think you're a witch," you say boldly. "Why, not at all."

And with that, you walk courageously toward the door.

"WELL, I AM!" the old woman yells.

And in a flash you are turned into a clucking chicken.

*Turn to page 30.*

"Time for breakfast! Time for breakfast!"
It's your mother calling. It was all a dream!
No fire, no witches. Just a beautiful summer day!

## The End

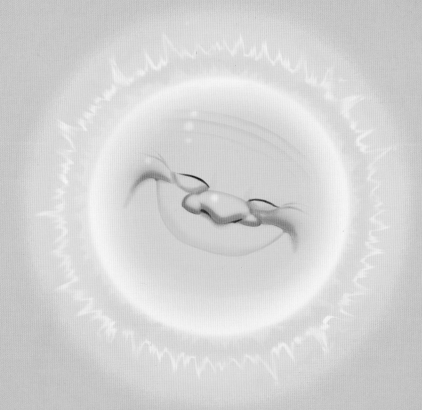

"Help me! My house is burning!" you say. "Can I use your phone?"

"Certainly, child," says Mrs. Ryerson. She shows you to the phone in the hallway, and you make the call. You remember to say exactly who you are and where you live.

"We'll be right there. Don't worry," says the fire fighter over the phone.

You turn to the old woman.

"Do you live here by yourself? I mean, are you all alone?" you ask.

*Turn to page 34.*

Mrs. Ryerson nods. Soon she looks toward the road. Even before you hear the sounds of the siren, she has seen the red truck speeding down the road.

"Look, child, the fire will soon be out. Don't worry. Now go on back home and watch them. You can come back another time if you'd like to visit."

*Turn to page 36.*

Later that day when the fire in your stove is safely out and your mom is home, you cross the road and fields to the old house again.

The door is closed, but this time you're not afraid. You knock, wait a bit, and knock again.

After a minute, the door opens.

"Why, child, I didn't expect you back so soon," Mrs. Ryerson says, smiling.

"I just want to thank you. My mom does, too. It was nice of you to help us," you say. "My mom and I want to know if you could come to dinner with us tomorrow. My dad can pick you up in the car. We'd really like it if you'd come."

"Why, yes, I'd like that, too. It's been a long time since I've been out."

Not only have you helped save your house, but you've also made a new friend.

**The End**

You drag the hose close to the house.

You've decided to put the fire out yourself. It's scary. Smoke is everywhere. You wish you hadn't decided to try this on your own!

The hose is just long enough to reach the kitchen window. You try to open the window.

It's locked!

"What do I do now?" you ask yourself. You can't go back inside the house. That's too dangerous. Maybe you should break the window.

You pitch a big rock through it. Black smoke pours out through the broken glass.

*Turn to page 40.*

You aim the hose at the window, but the stream of water is awfully thin.

"This is dumb! It won't work," you say out loud.

Just at that very moment, a fire truck, siren blaring, screeches to a halt on the road in front of your house. Six fire fighters in fire hats and rubber coats jump from the truck.

*Turn to page 62.*

You'd better get going to the firehouse. You could never put the fire out by yourself.

Nipper scrambles back down and you head off again on the bike. You pedal as hard as you can. A couple of cars pass you. You wish they would stop, but they don't know about the fire.

It's a long way to the firehouse up the hill.

Your muscles feel as though they are on fire, but you keep on pedaling. You make it to Fiddlers Pond. It's the halfway mark. Now comes the steep part of the hill.

*Turn to page 27.*

You dash to the nearest store. It's the bakery owned by Alice. She's a friend of yours.

"Help, Alice! Our house is on fire!" you yell.

Alice is out from behind the counter in seconds.

"Your house is on North Road, isn't it?" she asks.

"Yes. Hurry!" you answer.

*Turn to the next page.*

"Don't worry," Alice says. "I'm the fire chief. We're on our way! Nobody in the house, is there?"

You shake your head. "Nope, not even our cat."

When you get home, who is there but your mom! The smoke has begun to clear. She sees you and runs to you.

"I was so worried. Thank heavens you're all right!" You hug each other.

*Turn to page 48.*

Meanwhile, the fire fighters have searched the house. Now they're outside rolling up their hoses. They never even had to use the water. It was bread baking in the oven that caused the trouble. Aside from the smoke and probably a new paint job in the kitchen, everything's okay!

"You were so brave to ride to town and get the fire department," your mother says to you, giving you an extra hug.

## The End

You have to find the alarm fast. There must be one right in the firehouse.

But the door is locked! You can't believe it.

How can you—or anyone else—sound an alarm?

You turn the doorknob to the right and tug.

No good! You twist it to the left. No good again. You give the door a quick kick. That hurts!

*Turn to the next page.*

"Don't panic," you tell yourself. "Think clearly."
You slow down and look.

Right next to the locked door of the firehouse is a bright red metal box. It says in big silver letters:

FIRE ALARM
PULL HANDLE DOWN

*Turn to page 55.*

"I'm getting out of here," you say out loud.

You take off as fast as you can across the unmowed lawn, the fields, and the road.

You get back to your house just as your mom's car pulls up.

"Mom, I saw a witch! A real witch, Mom! Over there, over there at the house—"

"No time for that now. Our house is burning!" your mother says.

Just then the fire truck roars into the driveway.

Two fire fighters smash the living room window with axes. Smoke rushes out. It stings your eyes and makes you choke.

*Turn to page 20.*

The old woman at the door speaks again.
"Do you think I'm a witch? You aren't the first to think that. You do think that, don't you?"

*If you answer no, turn to page 28.*

*If you answer yes, turn to page 56.*

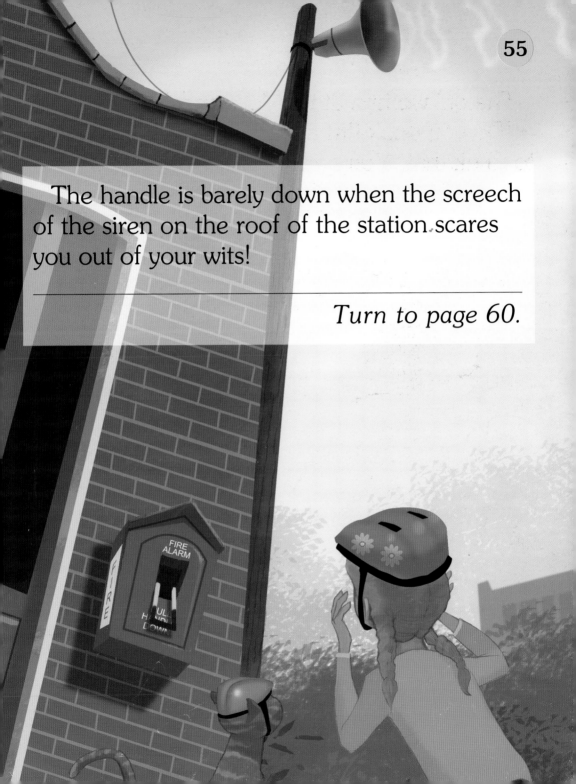

The handle is barely down when the screech of the siren on the roof of the station scares you out of your wits!

*Turn to page 60.*

"Why—umm—well—it's hard to say, ma'am. In a way, I guess you are a witch. But a nice witch, a very nice witch."

The old woman laughs softly.

"You're a brave one, you are. And an honest one at that. Sorry, though. I'm just a lonely old lady. Most kids run away from me. They're scared. But you're different."

*Go to the next page.*

You don't know quite what to say. At that moment, sirens scream on two fire trucks that are heading for your house. Someone in a passing car must have reported the fire.

"It's my house that's on fire. I've got to go! Bye," you say.

*Turn to the next page.*

You run home. You get there just in time to see the fire being put out.

What a day!

## The End

Within minutes, volunteer fire fighters are dashing out of stores and the houses in town.

*Turn to page 64.*

"We'll take care of this!" one of them yells. The others drag the heavy hose to your door.

*Turn to page 66.*

A friend of yours, Alice, runs out of the bakery she owns. She dashes over to you and asks, "Where's the fire?" She wears a hat that says Chief.

You tell her, and moments later you are in a fire truck, roaring down the road to your house.

You helped to stop the fire!

## The End

Soon the fire is out!

"Close call, kid. The biggest damage is to the bread baking in the oven." You look at the fire chief. She's the woman who owns the bakery in town.

"Bread? Just bread burning? That's all?" you say.

*Go on to the next page.*

The chief smiles and says, "Your mom probably forgot it. We'll wait till she gets back. It's lucky your neighbor called us! Why don't you come down and join us some Thursday night when we practice? We like junior fire fighters. I bet you'd make a good one."

## The End

# ABOUT THE ILLUSTRATOR

**Illustrator Keith Newton** began his art career in the theater as a set painter. Having talent and a strong desire to paint portraits, he moved to New York and studied fine art at the Art Students League. Keith has won numerous awards in art such as The Grumbacher Gold Medallion and Salmagundi Award for Pastel. He soon began illustrating and was hired by Walt Disney Feature Animation where he worked on such films as *Pocahontas* and *Mulan* as a background artist. Keith also designed color models for sculptures at Disney's Animal Kingdom and has animated commercials for Euro Disney. Today, Keith Newton freelances from his home and teaches entertainment illustration at the College for Creative Studies in Detroit. He is married and has two daughters.

# ABOUT THE AUTHOR

**R. A. Montgomery** attended Hopkins Grammar School, Williston-Northhampton School and Williams College where he graduated in 1958. Montgomery was an adventurer all his life, climbing mountains in the Himalaya, skiing throughout Europe and scuba-diving wherever he could. His interests included education, macro-economics, geo-politics, mythology, history, mystery novels and music. He wrote his first interactive book, *Journey Under the Sea*, in 1976 and published it under the series name *The Adventures of You*. A few years later Bantam Books bought this book and gave Montgomery a contract for five more, to inaugurate their new children's publishing division. Bantam renamed the series *Choose Your Own Adventure* and a publishing phenomenon was born. The series has sold more than 260 million copies in over 40 languages.

**For games, activities, and other fun stuff, or to write to Chooseco, visit us online at CYOA.com**

# Watch for these titles coming up in the

## CHOOSE YOUR OWN ADVENTURE®

## Dragonlarks® series for Beginning Readers

SEARCH FOR THE DRAGON QUEEN
DRAGON DAY
RETURN TO HAUNTED HOUSE
THE LAKE MONSTER MYSTERY
ALWAYS PICKED LAST
YOUR VERY OWN ROBOT
YOUR VERY OWN ROBOT GOES CUCKOO-BANANAS
THE HAUNTED HOUSE
SAND CASTLE
LOST DOG!
GHOST ISLAND
THE OWL TREE
YOUR PURRR-FECT BIRTHDAY
INDIAN TRAIL
CARAVAN
GUS VS. THE ROBOT KING
SPACE PUP
FIRE!
PRINCESS ISLAND

"In a world where children have so little autonomy, my children found delight as they were given the choice to create their own adventure. . . . Fun! Fun! Fun!"

— cyoa.com

"My seven-year-old son was captivated by the idea that he could have a hand in guiding a story about having his very own robot. The story lines kept my son reading over and over. Well done!!!"

— cyoa.com

Purchase online at www.cyoa.com or ask your local bookseller